STRANGER SEX COLLECTION

EXPLICIT DIRTY EROTICA SHORT STORIES

ARIELLE FOSSETT

plicit Press

CHAPTER 1

WANING LIGHT

STRONG HANDS, rough with calluses, ran over the princess's skin and she writhed under his touch.

This was why she'd come to the outermost regions of her kingdom, far from the responsibilities of being heir to one of the largest kingdoms in the world. Thousands of men wanted to bed the Balsikian princess. Most of them were nobility seeking to curry favor by pleasuring her. Here, in the tiny town of Carsep, the men had no delusions of what a night with the princess would mean.

Kaiya was two hundred and fifty years old, a child by Balsikian royalty standards, but for those without noble blood, reaching such an age was an impossibility. The more common the ancestry, the shorter the lifespan. Those in places like Carsep and its surrounding villages would be lucky to reach a hundred and fifty. The blacksmith apprentice currently between her legs was just under half a century and already looked the same age as she did. With flame-red hair and bright green eyes, Trekk was one of the most handsome men in Carsep, but also one of the poorest, limiting his options for marriage.

Those who could please Balsikian royalty in bed could choose virtually anyone to marry and Trekk had his sights set on a wealthy widow. But because he was merely an apprentice, he felt he didn't stand a chance against the other suitors without something to set him apart. When he'd come to Kaiya with his plight, she'd agreed to help almost immediately.

He'd feigned confidence when he'd approached her, but once she'd showed up at the small room he had above the shop, he'd fallen silent. Once inside, Kaiya had lowered her hood, revealing the elaborate and heavy braids of dark blue hair that marked her as not just royalty but a member of the ruling family of Balsik. Her pale gray eyes had sparkled with amusement when she'd seen Trekk swallow hard. When she'd dropped her cloak, his face had visibly paled.

She'd worn nothing beneath the cloak other than her boots. Kaiya was tall, just a few inches shorter than Trekk, her waist trim and limbs toned from years of exercise. As the only child of the Balsik king and queen, she'd been privileged to receive the same training as a prince would have, giving her a firmer body than she would've had otherwise. Her breasts were full; her nipples were milk chocolate against her otherwise pale skin. The hair between her legs was sparse, a shade of blue uniform with the braids that hung down her back.

It wasn't until Kaiya had kicked off her boots and started to remove Trekk's shirt that he'd broken from his frozen state and started to help. His trousers had fallen to the ground to reveal a long, thick manhood that swelled the instant she wrapped her hand around it. That touch had been what he'd needed to realize that this was really happening. All hesitation disappeared and he'd pulled Kaiya to him for a thorough and knee-buckling kiss.

Now, he was using that same technique to bring Kaiya to what promised to be the first of many orgasms. His fingers wrapped around her hips to hold her down as his tongue delved deep inside, coaxing her body to a higher place. When he moved his lips up to her little bundle of nerves, she cried out, back arching. Her hands went to her breasts, fingers rolling her nipples into hard points. She'd had many lovers over the years – Balsikians encouraged sexual exploration once a child reached sexual maturity – but none had been quite so skilled with their mouths as this one. As he sucked on her clit, he slid a finger inside, sending a new wash of sensations over her. When a second finger joined the first, Kaiya cried out again, her body shuddering with another climax.

"Inside me," the words were a half command, half plea. Her fingers raked through his thick hair, tugging at it.

Trekk was smiling as he rose over her. His mouth descended on hers and she tasted herself on his tongue. His palms skimmed over her breasts and she shivered. Their eyes met, green and gray darkened with desire, and she felt him against her entrance, hard and ready. Kaiya nodded, her hands running down Trekk's back to his muscular ass. Her body trembled with anticipation, and it was all she could do to keep from flipping them, sinking down on the massive erection she could feel between her legs, and riding the blacksmith until he popped.

As if he knew exactly what she was thinking, Trekk reached between them and took himself in hand. He rubbed the head over her clit and she whimpered, limbs twitching. She bit her lip to keep from begging. A princess did not beg, not even if she was sure she was going to combust if she didn't get something inside her right then. But if he didn't fuck her soon, she was going to have to seriously consider changing her stance on begging.

And then he was pushing his way inside her, forcing a noise out of her that she didn't recognize. Her eyes rolled back in her head, her body struggling to absorb the conflicting sensations racing across her nerves. The stretch was almost too much, just this side of painful, and her hips moved – whether to push him deeper or away, she wasn't entirely sure. Then he was in and moving and the whole world narrowed down to the flames licking across her body.

His strokes were slow and deep, each one rubbing across that spot inside that made her keen. The third started an orgasm that rolled over her, one wave after another until she was unable to tell when one ended and the next began. She dug her nails into his flesh, and his hips stuttered. She raised her head, lips against the shell of his ear.

"Now," she clenched her muscles around him and bit down on his earlobe.

He groaned as his body went rigid, his seed spilling into her. Kaiya wrapped her arms around him, pulling him down on her. As he slipped from between her legs, she made a small sound, a mini climax passing through her exhausted body. She closed her eyes, body limp and sated. Her mind was pleasantly blank, and her limbs turned to jelly. All of the pressures and responsibility were gone; the stress that had been tightening her body for weeks vanished. It would return, she knew, but for now, she was content.

CHAPTER 2

CUM AND RUN

THE ROUGH BARK bit into her upper back and shoulders but Rylee Keller didn't care. The sting of pain, the knowledge that anyone could walk by at any time, all of it just blended with the extraordinary sense of fullness, the delicious friction between her legs, sending her body into overload.

That morning when Rylee had left her apartment just after sunrise, she'd never imagined that her daily run in Sunset Park would end with her up against a tree, shorts, and underwear hanging off one ankle as it hooked around the waist of the hot stranger she'd been seeing on the trail for the past month. No, that morning, she'd had more mundane things on her mind.

Should she cut her shoulder-length bronze curls into a more manageable style? How was she going to decorate her third-grade classroom this upcoming fall? Was it finally time to trade in her 1999 Skylark? Were the eye drops going to get rid of the insomnia-induced redness in her smoky blue eyes before tonight's dinner with her parents?

She'd seen him, of course, when she got out of her car.

Ash blond hair, light green eyes, and a pretty boy face with full lips that, on a woman or a gay man, would've been referred to as 'cock- sucking' lips. He was the same height as she was – him just under average height, her just over – and had an athlete's build. Not the bulk of a football player or weightlifter. No, he was definitely more of a soccer or base-ball build. Just enough muscles for her to know that he could keep up with her and would have no problem going for hours, but not so much that he looked like he was over-compensating. More than once she'd found herself wondering what lay under those black mesh shorts and perfectly fitted t-shirts, and this time had been no exception. He'd smiled at her as she passed even white teeth that flashed against his tanned skin. They'd never actually spoken, but she'd heard a friend call him Tarik.

The tip of his ten-inch cock bumped against her cervix and Rylee cried out, mind rocketing back to the present. Tarik pulled the leg she wasn't standing on higher around her waist and changed the angle of penetration. Rylee dug her nails into Tarik's broad shoulders and he hissed, sliding his hands up her ribcage, up under her tank top. She whim-pered as Tarik shoved her sports bra up over her breasts, thumbs brushing across her sensitive nipples. Her insides began to quiver as each stroke sent ripples of pleasure across her nerves.

Her mind was racing, reeling, trying to absorb every-thing that had happened over the past two hours. Her run had been uneventful, but upon returning to her car, she'd found her pockets empty. Tarik had offered to help her look and they'd ventured back up the trail. Then, before she had been able to process it, Tarik's lips had been on hers, his tongue seeking access even as he'd pulled the two of them off the trail just enough to be out of sight. His mouth had been hot and demanding, his hands eager and Rylee's body had responded.

Now, his hips were pumping into her in a slow, steady rhythm as if he knew exactly how to play her body as if he knew just what to do to drive her nuts. They'd still barely spoken to each other, but Rylee could feel a connection. Even if it was just this one encounter, just a quickie with a stranger, it didn't feel like it to her. The moment their eyes had met, she'd felt like she knew him. She'd seen it on his face too and knew that even if they never saw each other again, they'd remember this encounter.

Rylee dropped one hand and flicked her finger over her clit, crying out as she came. When his fingers pinched her nipples, her body shook, the jolt enough to make her swear. It was almost too much to bear.

And then he was pulling out, cock hard and swollen with need. She let herself drop to her knees, hands instinctively resting on his hips as she leaned forward to take him in her mouth. The flavors exploded across her tongue, making her moan. Her own salty tang, the darker musky taste of him.

He let her be in control as she began to use her hand and mouth to bring him to his release. She felt the muscles under her left-hand jump and twitch as Tarik fought not to thrust. She sucked at the tip, sheathing her teeth as she drew more of the steel length into her mouth. Most girls would've just jerked him off or been less than enthusiastic about giving a blowjob to a cock that had just come from their pussy, but Rylee had always enjoyed giving head and didn't really mind her own taste. She loved the way she could make a man come apart, the way his face would look when she peered up at him. Some women thought of it as degrading, but Rylee understood the trust that came with wrapping her lips around such a sensitive piece of flesh.

"Rylee," his voice was strained as he warned her.

She didn't have to think about it. She hollowed out her cheeks, sucking hard as her hand worked over his thick shaft. It wasn't long before he came, spilling himself over her tongue. She swallowed, letting her mouth milk out every last drop.

Rylee couldn't bring herself to look at Tarik as she straightened her bra and tank top, or as she pulled up her underwear and shorts. Out of the corner of her eye, she could see Tarik tucking himself back into his shorts and picking up his t-shirt from where he'd tossed it. He stepped back up to the trail, pausing just on the other side of the tree line.

As she started after him, he called out, "Hey, I found your keys." He had them in his outstretched hand when Rylee stepped out onto the path. "They were about three feet further up."

"Thanks," Rylee took them, feeling the heat blaze in her cheeks. She stood there for another awkward minute before heading back to her car.

Tarik watched her walk away, admiring her firm ass. Next time, he fully intended to get a piece of that too. He'd need a bit more time and a better place than the park. He started to stroll back down the path. Stealing her keys had been good enough for a quickie. Maybe next time he would let the air out of her tire. Nothing to ruin it. Just enough of a problem to give him the opportunity to take her home... and to bed.

CHAPTER 3

BARNSTORMING SEX

MISS TESSA NICOLETTE WHITLEY'S mocha brown hair streamed in the wind as she flew her biplane, The Rogue Rage, over the fields. This was her first time examining France's vast farmlands. She smiled and looked down over the side at the tiny blue barn; her aero odometer read 1875, twenty-five miles from the ground. On her left, strapped like a pirate patch, her black band pink lens monocle-goggle spun around automatically adjusting the zoom few and colors heightened the colors. Her goggles blinked "possible alien abduction taking place in a barn."

Miss Tessa Whitley loved to travel time. She used to air race. Time jumping provided more excitement. She never knew what she'd encounter as a single French woman, no boyfriend or husband held her back. She didn't need to cook meals for any children. She made a Ferris wheel loop. At the apex of the circle, her engine cut off, as expected. Miss Tess Whitley loved danger. She kept turning the Rogue Rage until it dove downward, downward moving faster than an eagle. She leveled the Rogue Rage at twelve feet and flew in beside the barn. The flat grassland around the barn made a smooth landing.

She hopped out. She wore a brown leather flight jacket; black jockey's riding pants, black lace-up ankle boots, and a pink girly blouse with a huge white bow on the front. She bent forward low and let her long mocha tresses fall over toward the ground. Then she whipped her hair and head backward as she rose. "Perfect." Her hair was now very presentable in case she met a man.

She didn't hear anything.

Her goggles flashed again. "Alien abduction imminent!"

Miss Tessa frowned. Her monocle-goggles accuracy rate never fell below ninety-seven percent. Suddenly she heard a loud scream. A man's scream.

"HELP! HELP!"

Miss Tessa's time ring, a gold-jeweled band with several spinning gears in the center covered by a blue dome decorated in black notches, spun wildly. "Another life form present." Miss Tessa sprinted, splashing puddles of rain, and squished cow chips and squashing the rich green grass. She pulled out her Steam Laser Pistol from her green messenger bag as she neared the blue barn door. She yanked the door open. The horrible scene unfolded before her blue eyes.

"HELP IT GOT ME!" the man screamed.

Miss Tessa Whitely saw a wiry, intellectual looking man, a professor of some sort in a black jacket, pants and a white shirt clenching tightly to a barn stall. His body was wrapped in thin noodle-like pink tentacles encircling his legs, arms, shoulders, chest, neck and now his face. The man wasn't strong enough to resist such a creature. Few would have been able to free themselves.

To make matters worse, the female horse in the stall kicked wildly against the stall door trying to protect herself. Between each horseback kick, the man quickly adjusted to save his fingers from being crushed.

Miss Tessa's eyes faced the alien creature. It stood eight feet away in the barn. Round pink blob about the size of the barn door. One eye focused on the man. This eye had a large blue pupil.

Below is a hungry-looking mouth opening and closing repeatedly. In between these is an indented nose.

He wore a fashionable hairstyle of the day, black hair, parted down the middle and curled up on both sides. His oval face contorted in agony, straining against the creature. Dodging the horse's lightning bolt hoof kicks. He finally let go to save his hands from being smashed into obliteration.

His heels tried to dig into the dirt. His hands clawed at the pink tentacles. All was useless. He was efficiently dragged slowly toward the Pink Blob-Eye creature's furnace-like mouth.

Miss Tessa aimed her Steam Laser Pistol. Through her Monocle-goggles a messaged flashed. "Aim between the alien's eye and indented nose." Miss Tessa pulled the trigger. A brief spurt of steam erupted from her gun top and a blue laser beam hit the creature right in between its eye and nose. Rope snapping sounds and a high shriek emerged from the creature. It let go.

It fell flat to the ground. Miss Tessa put her hand to her mouth. "Hideous." She said seeing how the Pink Blob-Eye's front side looked exactly like the same on its backside. It puffed up one last time and deflated into a pink pool with streams of pink flowing from all around. Miss Tessa stored her Steam Pistol back inside her green messenger bag, strapped across her buxom D cup chest.

Miss Tess rushes to the man. She helped him onto his feet.

"I can't thank you, enough!" he said in a German accent. "I'm Professor Everett Lucas Stoneham, Discover-Photographer-Historian. I was investigating noises reported in this barn. I investigate alternative life forms from other worlds. Now we have some small proof they exist," he pointed to the quickly fading pink blob, turning red-brown like the barn dirt.

"I'm Miss Tessa Nicolette Whitley. Stunt flyer, wing walker. I can fly any kind of plane, cargo planes, spitfires, jets, biplanes, seaplanes, or aerostat balloons. I fly the Rogue Rage, my biplane, and travel around investigating the time frame 1770s to the 1900s.

The Professor replied shocked, "You travel in the future?" He pointed to his watch. "All over the world." Miss Tessa replied.

"What's that monocle on your eye?"

"Calculating machine. Except it holds data and images from various travels I've been on." "I think I'm in love."

"I'm a modern French woman. Sex is more practical. I use birth control.'" "But where?"

Miss Tessa pushed Professor Stoneham into a dry horse stall. She quickly disrobed her horse-riding pants, blouse, jacket, and boots in a messy pile on the hay floor.

He didn't allow her to beat him as they raced to get naked.

Seconds later, she stood three feet from him. Her twenty-seven-year-old vanilla white skin was flawless. Her massive heavy boobs showed, uncovered by the flight jacket and freed from the blouse. Her hips swayed as she approached his wiry intellectual frame. "I knew you were a professor. Soon as I saw your body."

"I know how to keep it up." He said, diving straight for Miss Tessa's boob flesh. "I've read the Kama Sutra from India."

Miss Tessa dragged him down onto the hay. She pulled him on top of her. Her long hair got messy, but she didn't care. Professor Stoneham lay between her quivering legs. "I am all wet and gooey inside Professor. Fuck me. Now!"

Professor Stoneham entered her abruptly wasting no time. He was a man who just faced death. His senses heightened. His every nerve is aware of Miss Tessa's femininity. He sank down into her sex grotto and as his dick grew wetter and wetter, he let out a satisfying sigh.

Miss Tessa's thighs went high around the Professor's mid-back. She gave him a leg hug tighter than a bear hug and started using his long cock to stir up her cunt fluids. He was a stranger, but they had so much in common. She really could envision a long-term relationship between them.

She reached up and fed the Professor her huge elongated breast. She reached down and fondled his pool-size man sacs. "I love it when a man has big balls."

. . .

"I'm a rutting horse," professor Stoneham replied. He began shoving his hard, hot big cock inside her pussy slot faster and faster. The hay squeaked. The sound of scuffling in the next stall made the female horse whinny and snort.

Miss Tessa's cunt hole stroked Professor Stoneham's pussy splitter from tip to root and back. Until finally, she held him tightly wrapped in her legs and arms. They both came and released their fuck fluids into and onto each other.

They got dressed. "When we time travel we need code names to always remember each other. You can call me Veva."

"Hmmmm. You can call me Maxwell Octavius Ashdown."

That decided, the two planned on investigating the time from 1770s to 1900s some more.

Miss Tessa revved her biplane's engine. The Rogue Rage's propeller wings dull sound started chopping the air. Faster the propellers spun. Miss Tessa smiled. "Hold on Professor. I'll show you 1879 in a few minutes." Her biplane roared down over the flat grassland. After some twenty feet, the Rogue Rage veered upward and into the blue sky.

"Maybe one day we can get married," Professor Stoneham suggested, holding onto the biplane side as it made a sharp turn into what looked like thick clear heat waves.

"In the future, Professor," she pointed to the time waves approaching them. "In the future."

CHAPTER 4

CYBER BOOTY CALL

YVONNE WAS a dark and tall combination of a sassy attitude and sexy seductiveness. Standing at 5'9 with tan skin, dusky brunette shoulder-length hair, and pretty brown eyes, she knew exactly what to do in order to get a man to say yes to spending an evening together. It wasn't hard. After so many years of being taught the art of sex by the best females, she felt like an expert. Still, sometimes she didn't know what she was getting her head into with these special meetings she arranged. So far, she had been safe, but she knew that any woman in her position was putting themselves at a risk.

Yvonne wasn't a prostitute. She didn't sell her body for sex, nor did she justify anyone else doing the same either. She wasn't a madam, nor was money any part of the equation when she had a sexual encounter. What she was, though, and what she knew she was from her heart and mind, was that she was a pro. There was no one that could do what she could do, and that was why so many of them kept coming back, spreading the word so that others could get a sample taste as well.

It was dusk. Yvonne had finished doing her makeup. She had been perusing some ads and placing some ads online. She loved the risk of adventure, the love for lust. It was sexual hunting. Casual encounters. She would have her fun this Halloween. All dressed up for the occasion in long fishnet stockings and a witch's hat, she knew exactly who to expect at 8:30. Well, she hoped that her expectations would line up well with the picture he had emailed her and the information he had given her. Sometimes the guys lied. Oh well. From what she saw face, body, and cock wise- she was pretty sure that she wouldn't be disappointed.

There were still emails coming in but Yvonne put them away for now. The doorbell was ringing.

Her new partner for the evening had come. John, he had called himself in the email. Who cared if it was real or not?

Yvonne made her way to the door, softly walking with her hand outstretched to grab the doorknob. She stopped before she just opened it so carelessly. This would be better if she stalled and played with the surprise.

"Who is it?" she asked innocently. "John," the voice said with a ring to it.

Yvonne smirked playfully like a cat ready to play. With

a graceful hand, she opened the door to see John standing there, smiling with the same playful smirk, a powerful twinkle in his eyes. So far, she was not disappointed. His face was just like it was in the photos- short, curly brown hair, beautiful blue eyes, and a square jaw that wasn't too much of a box. He had a strong jaw but a gentle face as well.

Standing at 6'4, he was a good enough height, and his thick but healthy muscular frame was enough to handle Yvonne. She just had to get him out of those jeans, that blue shirt, and trench coat...

"Why, John," Yvonne said with a smile. "So good of you to come by." Immediately, she reached for his hand and pulled him in.

Before she could say 'have a seat', John had pounced on her. This was exactly what she wanted- there would be no need for niceties or stalling- John would get what he was craving now. He could probably already smell her pussy in the air; she had been hot and wet in anticipation. Luckily, the door had been closed and locked before he picked Yvonne up and walked her to the sofa. His hands had already reached into her underwear. Yvonne cried out as he kissed her deeply and passionately, swapping back spit and moving tongue against tongue. They could taste each other as their mouths meshed, and Yvonne had already started to unzip her new partner. She could feel his massive length through his underwear and she could already tell that the cock was going to match the pictures she saw, even before he would put it inside of her. Both of them were very aroused.

. . .

Yvonne pointed to her staircase, taking a breather from the kissing. "Please... John... can we take this to my room?"

John didn't need much convincing. With his shoes and socks thrown on top of his jeans, the bare-legged John started to march up the stairs. Yvonne held securely in his arms- God, she thought, he was so strong! She wasn't used to a lot of guys being able to hold her like that since she was a pretty tall and tough cookie herself.

Yvonne felt herself getting tossed on the bed. Without much left to be said, her lingerie was thrown to the side. John mounted her, starting to rub up against her arms and skin, kissing her delicately on her nipples. Yvonne moaned. She was already fingering and playing with her cunt, but it wasn't long before she had to remove her hand for John's cock. His dick started to take control of her pussy, pushing in and letting his balls swing underneath. His hands held the woman down as he pressed into her. At first, Yvonne worried because she could tell that John wasn't wearing a condom. Then again, she remembered- they had talked about it. John was clean, and she trusted him. Either that, or fuck it, she didn't care. Besides, she was on birth control.

The cock was already starting to hurt, but it felt good at the same time. Yvonne knew she could ignore the pain, so she just dealt with it the best way she could. She was moaning, taking the cock in inch by inch. She was impressed. John was stretching her pussy like a rubber band. The more she got comfortable and used to the fucking, John would seem to slide a little bit deeper, hurting Yvonne again. She had always felt like such a pro! Then again, the guys she had fucked probably hadn't had the length or width of a cock like John's. Yvonne had a feeling that she was going to be put to shame- in a good way.

"Take it," John said as his partner moaned loudly. "Take it, like a good fuck."

Yvonne was turned on immensely. She had never been called a good fuck before! She was really getting into it now, and the pain was less of a restriction. She could press against her partner now, shove her cunt further on his dick, grip her hands to his skin, and press as hard as she could. She could feel herself dripping on her bed covers, her teeth biting against her lip, and her head pressed back. Yes, she was screaming, yes, yessssssss...

John smiled as he fucked his new play buddy. He really liked the feel and texture of her cunt. He could tell that she fucked often- the pussy definitely wasn't tight or hard to penetrate. At the same time, he could feel it opening more and more. He had to wonder if she had ever been fucked like this before. No way- he was the best. He knew. He was a pro, and he knew how to fuck a cunt. This one was nice, wet and slippery. Only a joker would need lubrication for it- the pussy basically juiced itself perfectly. It wasn't drying out anytime soon, but he could sure tell by the look on Yvonne's face that she

was nearing a climax. The pussy felt so good, and John could tell, from how it gripped his cock, that he would be reaching orgasm as well.

They both did, at the exact same time. John made a face of passion that she found adorable. Yvonne gave a gaping, loud moan. With a few more thrusts, John could feel Yvonne's pussy steadily pouring over him before he pulled out. They were both dripping on each other, on the bed, in puddles and little streams.

Yvonne laid back on her bed, moaning to herself as John started to walk down the stairs. She wanted to say something real fun yet momentous. "God, you're perfect," maybe, or, "wow, baby... you sure know how to work that stick." But as she could hear him shuffling downstairs, putting his clothes on before walking down the door, she thought to herself. Was it really that serious? No, she got what she wanted, and he got what he wanted. It was a cyber booty call, nothing more and nothing less, on a beautiful and wild Halloween night.

Yvonne wasn't a whore. She wasn't a slut, or even a sex fiend. She was a professional woman, a woman that knew what she wanted, and she respected John as an equal, one looking for the same.

. . .

Rising from her bed, Yvonne headed for the shower. After washing up, she would go to the costume party she had planned to go to. The next day, she would resume her normal hunting schedule as usual.

CHAPTER 5

LAZY BOUTIQUE SEX
(REBOUND STRANGER SEX)

SOME PEOPLE WIN the lottery and some people have rebound sex. I'm a rebound sex kind of girl. I broke up with Brad for playing around with me. I don't have to take that shit. I look like a fucking Goddess on Victoria's Secret runway. I've got a long lean shape all the boys want to fuck. The girls envy my easy-going self-confidence. And my cunt juices up are real hot when I find a boy I like. My cunt always makes the right choices. So when I kicked Brad out, I placed my ad in the college paper. It read, "roommate wanted: senior, mature, capable of handling household responsibilities". I was surprised when Ty showed up on my doorstep. Ty is an African American, studying Rubber Goods Production at a local Vocational-Tech university.

Ty's awesome figure, muscles small enough to hug a girl, and bright white teeth smile won me over big. He said he loved building things. And as a rubber good production worker, cleaning up came second nature to him. The five-foot-eight-inch hunk already had a job! He worked nights. He worked at the Baur Rubber Plant as an injection-molding machine tender. He makes all kinds of rubber products from gloves, to diapers, balloons to dildos.

My pussy started dripping during the interview for the spare room in the house I rented.

He works nights mostly. I workdays. I thought we might enjoy some great sex, only to find out he is dedicated to his job and won't take a day off. I cannot miss my classes; so we remained virtual strangers for six months. His money orders for the rent and utilities always arrived on time. Slipped right under my bedroom door just before sunrise.

Having Ty a few feet away from me made finding another man impossible. I wanted Ty and I'm sure Ty wanted me. Ty became my rebound fuck guy.

That's how you do it, ladies. If you're going to fuck someone on the rebound, find someone local, a stranger, hot as can be.

One night during the spring, my cunt tingled and trembled. That's when I realized, Ty would be graduating soon. I'd be going back home to Montana! I had to do something.

I didn't want Ty to remain a stranger. I didn't want him to become a friend either. Rebound sex is not for friends, ladies!

My one chance arose on finals week. I didn't have regular classes, which meant I could be home when Ty returned from work. I rose early. I hopped into the shower. We share the same shower!

I was lathering up my three-day hair when I heard the door close. I heard the sound of heavy feet coming up the steps. The feet stopped at my door for a second. I remembered it was rent time. That must be Ty. I kept showering and put a nice leathering of hair shampoo on my pussy.

I stroked my pussy crack in and out, making myself hotter and hotter. I turned around facing the wall. Ty told me his routine. "Come home, take a shower, go to bed." I bent over and washed my legs. I acted like I was about to shave when the bathroom door opened.

Ty must have been really tired. Because he dropped all his work clothes, jeans, red and black checked cotton shirt. The nice smell of hot rubber filled the bathroom. He kept moving toward the foggy shower door, not hearing the water running. After all, I'm always fast asleep. And Ty works a ten-hour shift.

He opened the door and stepped into the shower, pinning my face toward the shower wall. Finally, he realized it as the hot steamy water hit his round smooth black face.

"Oh shit! Brandy what are you doing!"

"Taking a shower," I cooed. I turned around suds all over my modest B cup breasts. My long blonde hair was a dark brunette under the shower water. I had suds up between my legs. "I was about to shave my legs."

"I'm sorry," he apologized and quickly stepped out.

I grabbed his thick black arm. "Come here, stranger." I smiled, "It's time you and I got acquainted."

Ty relaxed and he stepped back inside, him and his boner.

"I splashed water on his strong chest and muscular hips. He had the biggest butt. I reached my hands around, hugged his waist, and groped his butt. "Just the kind of butt a white girl loved to hold while fucking."

"Mmm," he replied. His brown eyes grew bigger. His raging hard-on poked me in my uterus.

"I know a better way to get your hot ball juice inside my uterus," I purred.

Ty's large black hands cupped my apple-sized breasts. "I love breasts that curve upward, always ready to suck and lick." He lowered his black face to my hot nubs. I pushed my chest further, forcing my titties down his black mouth. I loved his hot tongue licking all around my breasts.

He licked under the creases of my breasts, where my boobs just started to sag this year.

Water rushed over our bodies and we grew slippery slick. Easily our hands glided over our aroused skin. My hands slipped down his strong back muscles. At last, I cupped his hard firm beefcakes. His hands slithered pasty my belly button jewelry, over my Venus mound, and into my pussy crack.

His thick fingers wasted no time penetrating me. "Brandy," he said hesitantly, excited and hot, "I've been fantasizing about fucking you. I thought you'd remain a stranger forever!"

"I'm right here Ty. Take me," I panted and raised one foot to the tub rim. My position gave his fuckpole, sticking straight out a straight path into my fuckhole. He pushed his groin forward. I gripped both his buttocks and brought us together like two gears in a machine shop. I leaned back and let the water run down my modest chest. Excited, I let go and Ty held me. He grabbed my perky butt cheeks. I thought I went to heaven when he pulled my ass cheeks apart, making his cock seem twice as big as it already was. His one-and-a-half-inch girth matched anything I'd previously had. He was an eyebrow's width short of nine inches long!

We thrashed and pushed until at last, his cockhead nudged my cervix. I didn't want him to move. "I have to move, Brandy. I need to feel your pussy ripple over my hot black flesh." He put it so nicely, so I started closing my pussy muscles on his wangpole on the outstroke. I relaxed and accepted his length and girth on the in-stroke. Every time the base of his cock touched my ruby pearl. I sighed.

We built up speed. Soon both of us shook back and forth like a washer and dryer. We rubbed our delicious skin over one another. I had a flood of juices inside my cunt. He churned inside me until I melted like butter. I came, exploding my girl sauce all over his dick sausage. His pussy driller spewed wet oily sperm all up my cooze.

When we came a second time, five minutes later, we relaxed and playfully showered one another. Satisfied, at last, we cut off the water.

I wrapped my towel around his waist.

Ty wrapped his towel around my breasts. We went into my room and fucked again.

I can't say Ty and I stayed together. But we had the best stranger fuck I've ever experienced.

ABOUT THE AUTHOR

Arielle Fossett is an emerging erotica author of many erotica kinks and sub-genres. Be sure to check out other books and leave a review if this story got you hot!

Visit my blog at Arielle Fossett's Blog

Join my newsletter for the exclusiveArielle Fossett's Newsletter

Sign up for Free Stories from Xplicit Press Authors

Xplicit Press Author Updates

Like Xplicit Press on Facebook

Follow Xplicit Press on Twitter

Readers: I want to expand a few of the stories to see where the characters can be explored further. If there are any of the stories that you would like to read more about again, I'd love to hear from you!

Keep In Touch
Arielle Fossett
info@ariellefossett.com